The Summer Stories

Kay Seeley

Published by

Enterprise Books

.

ISBN: 0993339492
ISBN-978-0-9933394-9-3:

TO: DARIEN AND TOBEY

WITH LOVE

.

Kay Seeley lives in London. She is a novelist, short story writer and poet.

Her short stories have been published in various magazines including: The People's Friend, Woman's Weekly, Yours, Take-a-Break and The Weekly News. Her stories have also been short-listed in several major competitions. She has written three Victorian novels which have all been selected as finalists in The Wishing Shelf Awards.

Kay's books:

The Water Gypsy

The Watercress Girls

The Guardian Angel

Also by Kay Seeley:

Short Story Collections

The Cappuccino Collection 20 stories to warm the heart

The Christmas Stories.

BOX SET

The Victorian Novels

CONTENTS

My Best Friend's Wedding

'I need a new dress,' I said to the girl in the shop. 'Something amazing, after all it's my best friend's wedding.'

Sophie had been my best friend since she sat next to me in primary school. She was a giggler and full of fun. We were always in trouble for chattering and laughing. We became known as the terrible two. I loved her like a sister. As we grew up we became inseparable – Sophie the head-turning blonde with legs up to her armpits, and me, the mousy-haired hanger-on happy to bask in her reflected glory. In our teens we'd hit the discos and clubs – Sophie sparkled and shone like a twinkling star while I hovered in her shadow. Not that I was bad looking, but next to Sophie anyone would pale into mundane insignificance. I didn't mind. Sophie was Sophie – a one off and I was glad to have her as my best friend. We even double-dated sometimes but deep inside I knew my partner only had eyes for Sophie.

Then she met Mark. Drop-dead gorgeous with dark hair made for running your fingers through and come-to-bed eyes that would melt lead at a hundred paces. He was witty, ambitious and charming, plus he drove a sports car. What more could any girl want? Sophie wanted him and she had an uncanny way of getting whatever she wanted. I'm not saying Sophie was shallow, but a saucer's got more depth.

Rugby matches and nights in the pub with Mark replaced our girl's nights out. I was relegated to days when Mark was unavailable or out of town. Not that I minded. I'd met Brian by then.

I was bridesmaid at their wedding. I wore pink and looked like a blancmange. Sophie looked like a princess. She glided down the Cathedral aisle like a ship in full sail with her train billowing out behind her. She glowed with happiness. The music swelled to the rafters. I was one of the ten bridesmaids following in her wake.

The wedding was the social event of the calendar. Sophie's dad was on the City Council and no expense was spared. If the cost of the wedding bore any relation to the longevity of the marriage it should have lasted a lifetime. But it didn't.

Within six months the cracks were beginning to show. Suddenly I was in demand again. 'He doesn't care about me,' Sophie complained. 'He spends more time at work than he does at home. We never go anywhere. He cares more about his algorithms and mega-bites than he does about me. Honest, I'm turning into a house-mouse. We never have any fun.'

'It's bound to feel a bit of a come-down after such a fantastic wedding,' I said. 'But you can't party forever. It's just post-wedding blues.'

But Sophie didn't agree. She'd dreamt of living life in the fast-lane and nothing less would do, while Mark was dedicated to building his own business.

'He wants me to get pregnant,' she said to me several months later. 'What does he think I am – some sort of cow? Oh, sorry.' I was pregnant with Kirsty at the time.

'Perhaps he just wants children?' I said. Sophie looked disgusted.

Yes, definitely a red dress. I was wearing red when I met Brian. It's his favourite colour. He was in the army then. I met him at a club when he was on leave. We got married soon after, before he went back to join his regiment. He was often away so I couldn't see what Sophie was moaning about. At least her husband came home every night – eventually.

By the time Brian left the army we had two children, Kirsty and Joe. Brian settled for a job as an electrician re-wiring people's houses. We were content, which is more than I can say about Sophie.

Her marriage spluttered on for a few more years but her heart wasn't in it. Before long she was a regular visitor for girls' nights in. During long wine-soaked evenings, when Mark was working, I had a full run down of his short-comings.

'All I want is a chance to go out and enjoy myself,' Sophie would say. I resisted the urge to point out that, with two small children, I wasn't exactly tearing up the dance floor or clubbing the night away either.

'I can't bear it,' she'd say. 'I'm married to an unfeeling robot. I want out.' And Sophie always got what she wanted.

I saw less of her after the divorce. She went a bit wild, like a garden without the gardener. A succession of men passed through her life but every time the break up came she was back. We'd drink wine and she'd cry on my shoulder all over again. She came round so often Brian asked when she was moving in. Sometimes she'd drink so much he had to drive her home. 'Why do I always fall for the wrong guy?' she'd ask.

Any port in a storm, I thought but said, 'You expect too much. They're only human.'

'I don't know what wrong with me,' she'd say. 'It's all right for you, you've got Brian.'

But I didn't have him for long did I? Not once Sophie set her beady eye and staple gun claws on him. I should have known.

'It's a second wedding,' I said to the girl as I flicked through the dresses on the rail in the shop. 'Not such a show-stopper as the first. It's in a Country Hotel.'

'If you want sensational they're over here,' the girl said leading me to a rail at the back.

Designer outfits from Prada, Dior, McQueen and Valentino shuffled along the rail beneath my hands. They were so gorgeous they took my breath away.

A knock-your socks-off, Electric Crimson number shimmered in my hand. It was so amazing I wanted to cry.

I tried it on. It was achingly beautiful. Short, clingy and low cut enough to be just this side of indecent. It was everything I could ever have hoped for and what's more it showed off my newly acquired tan brilliantly.

I stepped into a pair of killer heels and swirled my hair up on top of my head. I looked so hot Brian's eyes would melt. I'd show him what he's missing.

I'd show Sophie too, when I walk in with Mark. His dedication to work paid off. He's just sold his techno business for a couple of million. She'll turn green when she sees us, just back from our wedding on the beach and our honeymoon in Barbados. Eat-your- heart out Sophie. This time I'm getting what I want.

(First published in Take-a-Break Fiction Feast in 2014)

KAY SEELEY

Postman's Knock

Lisa rushed to open the door, even though she was still in her nightie. She'd worked late last night and slept in but didn't want to miss the post. Old Jimmy the post man was early; he didn't usually deliver until after eight and ringing the doorbell meant a parcel, a parcel containing the birthday present she'd ordered online. If she missed the delivery she'd have to trek into town to pick it up at the sorting office which she couldn't do until the weekend, so she'd be too late for her mum's birthday.

She was breathless as she hurried to the door. She was even more breathless when she opened it. Kerchow! Her mind spun. He was gorgeous! Dressed in his red post office uniform and orange Hi-Viz jacket he seemed to fill the doorway. A sprinkling of raindrops sparkled in his black as night hair making it shiny as jet, dark brown eyes surveyed her and, in a fleeting moment of madness, she had the overwhelming desire to have his babies. She was so struck by his looks all she could do was stand and stare for what felt like forever, until she realised he was staring back.

Suddenly she became aware of what she must look like; bare-legged, pasty-faced with bed-hair. Worse still, the words 'I Never Wear Knickers' were emblazoned in red on the front of her shorter than decent nightdress. It had been a joke present from her brother whose wild sense of humour was legendary and who'd dared her to wear it. That was when she was with her ex-boyfriend Marc who had no sense of humour at all. No wonder he was staring! Probably couldn't believe his eyes.

She swallowed, pulled herself up to her full height and said, 'Ah, a parcel,' as though it was the most natural thing in the world to see a gut-wrenchingly handsome example of masculinity on her doorstep at 6.30 in the morning and greet him wearing hardly anything at all.

He smiled and his eyes softened as they filled with mirth. 'There are letters too,' he said holding out some envelopes.

'Yes, of course,' she said taking them. Then, before she knew it he was gone and she could breathe again.

All through the day at work the vision of his face kept intruding into her brain and imposing itself on the faces around her. It was ridiculous, she told herself, but somehow she couldn't get him out of her mind. What must he have thought of her, pudding faced without make-up, blonde hair all awry and that nightdress!

That evening she sorted out the up-to-the-neck and down-to-the-ankles pale blue flannel nightgown her Nan had bought her. 'For those cold winter nights,' she had said.

Then she unearthed the cosy dressing gown Marc had left behind. She put a hairbrush and sick of lippy on the hall-stand, so, should he call again she'd be able to present a reasonable, at least half-decent image.

She was awake at six, heard the clock chime seven and decided to get up and make a cup of tea. Her feet had hardly touched the floor when the doorbell rang.

Adrenaline pulsed through her veins, butterflies sprang to life in her stomach and a broad smile stretched across her face as she rushed to open the door. In her haste she forgot about the dressing gown, hairbrush and lippy. She'd also forgotten how difficult it was to run in a full length flannel nightgown. The fabric wound itself around her legs and, as she opened the door she caught her foot in the hem and tipped forward propelling herself into the arms of the astonished postman. She breathed in the citrus tang of his aftershave and revelled in the solid safety of his muscular arms. Her eyes were on a level with his tantalisingly attractive jawline and goosebumps prickled her back. She'd fallen for him in a big way but hadn't meant to demonstrate it in such an obvious fashion.

'Oh God, sorry,' she said, her face burning hot enough to light a fire on an iceberg.

'My pleasure,' he said, helping her back to vertical. Laughter danced in his melting chocolate eyes and Lisa found herself covered in confusion all over again.

'One to sign for,' he said handing her the package and hand-held computer.

She took a couple of breaths to steady herself and signed her name as slowly as she could, taking the time to read the text on the computer screen. She swallowed. 'You're new aren't you? Haven't seen you round here before. What's happened to Jimmy, the old postman?'

'He had a bit of a fall,' he said. 'I'm filling in 'till he's back on his feet.'

'Oh,' she said, handing him back the computer.

'Have a nice day and mind that nightie doesn't trip you up again,' he said with a grin. He touched his hand to his forehead in farewell.

Lisa groaned as she shut the door. He must be laughing all the way to the post office, she thought. What a dork I must have looked.

Over the next week Lisa received at least one parcel every day. By the end of the week she had at least managed to get her act together and had brushed her hair and put some lippy on before she opened the door. Each day their doorstep exchanges became longer and more revealing. By the end of the week Lisa had found out that his name was Gareth, he lived alone, loved sport, went para-gliding at weekends and was saving up for a sports car. She still had collywobble knees, butterflies and trouble breathing whenever she saw him but a wave of pleasure would engulf her as she watched him walking up the front path.

In the middle of the week there were cards as well as packages. 'It's my birthday,' Lisa said when he pointed them out.

'Congratulations,' he said. 'Have a great day.'

'I will,' she said although she knew she wouldn't. She was working late again and the birthday drink she'd planed with her friend Becky had been cancelled as Becky was in bed with flu.

'You must have a lot of friends or are you running some sort of business?' he asked one day in the third week as he was delivering the umpteenth package.

'I've got lots of friends,' she said, which wasn't true either.

'Not that I'm complaining,' he said. 'I look forward to your deliveries. Such an interesting array of parcels. I can't imagine what's in them.'

'You'd be surprised,' she said and shut the door.

The following Monday morning as Lisa opened the door, no longer rushing as she knew he'd wait, she was surprised to see a woman carrying her letters and packages.

'Where's Gareth,' she asked, alarm clenching her stomach.

'Gareth?' the woman said. 'He'll not be back anytime soon.'

Lisa' heart dived into her slippers. Breath escaped her as her hopes and dreams fell like sparrows into the mud. The thought of never seeing him again filled her insides with dull aching sickness. Suddenly the days ahead felt empty and pointless. What had started as a jokey exchange on the doorstep had become meaningful and important and something she relied on to brighten up her day. She'd never missed anyone so much in her life. Tears filled her eyes.

'What happened?' she asked as the knot in her stomach tightened.

'He had an accident. Fell off a cliff. Nasty business,' the postwoman said shaking her head.

'But he's alright isn't he?' *Please say he's alright*, Lisa thought as a hundred dreadful scenarios whirred through her brain.

'Well, he's in hospital. Broke both legs. Be a while before he's back.'

Lisa sighed with relief.

It didn't take her long to find him at the hospital. He was on her list of new patients. He hadn't 'fallen off a cliff' as the postwoman put it, but he had landed badly while para-gliding and broken both his ankles. When she saw him lying there her heart fluttered. He was still gorgeous and now he was all hers.

'Hi,' she said as she walked up to his bed. 'I'm your physiotherapist. It looks as though we'll be spending lots of time together if I'm to get you back on your feet.'

Surprise followed by a broad grin lit up his face. 'Fantastic,' he said. 'I'll look forward to that. So there is an upside to broken ankles. I couldn't be in better hands.' The look in his eyes told Lisa he meant it.

All those hours online ordering things for next day delivery and sending them to herself over and over again had paid off. Now all she had to do was find homes for the stuff she'd bought and hopefully a new home for her hapless postman. 'Any questions?' she asked.

'Just one,' he said, his eyes sparkling with interest. 'That first nightie. Do you really '*Never Wear Knickers?*''

(First published in Take a Break Fiction Feast in 2015)

In Search of the Exotic

Kira gazed enviously at her sister Lisa's stunning orchid, its flower laden stem arching across the window. The red and orange richness of the centre and the white petal blooms appeared like a kaleidoscope of butterflies caught in flight. They looked so perfect she wondered if they were real. She reached out her hand to stroke the petals and felt their velvety softness. They were real all right.

'Lovely isn't it?'

Kira spun round to see Ollie, Lisa's husband standing behind her.

' Yes, I was just admiring it,' she said.

' That's the orchid I gave Lisa on our wedding day,' he said proudly. ' It's bloomed ever since. Just like our love for each other.' Kira didn't miss the satisfaction in his voice.

Kira sighed. She had been bridesmaid at her sister's wedding. It was three years ago now. How had Lisa managed to keep the orchid alive, yet alone in blossom all that time? Lisa had given Kira an orchid then too. A purple one. It only lasted three weeks. When the flowers fell and the leaves turned brown she'd thrown it in the bin.

She thought back to her other horticultural failures. The Peace Lily she forgot to water, the

Spider plant everyone said was easy to grow, but not if you go away on holiday and forget it, and the African Violet that never flowered until she gave it to her mum, who coaxed it into glorious bloom. But orchids? Well that was another kettle of fish. If Lisa had successfully kept one for three years, perhaps she could too.

When Lisa and Kira were growing up they had been fiercely competitive, each egging the other on and trying to outdo the others' achievements. Lisa was the eldest, good at sports and academically bright. Kira, on the other hand struggled, but she'd not be outdone, so, anything Lisa did, Kira did better or at least as well. She'd always thought orchids were a bit too exotic and fragile to keep as a houseplant herself, but Lisa had shown her how wrong she could be. Growing an orchid of her own presented itself as a challenge, and Kira was not one to back down from a challenge.

That afternoon, on her way home she popped into the florist. The shop was run by a cheerful, powdery lady who smelled of lavender. Kira knew her as Carrie. She'd done the flowers for Lisa's wedding, so Ollie must have bought Lisa's orchid here.

'I'm looking for an orchid, white flowers, hardy, long lasting,' she said when Carrie greeted her.

' An orchid? Well, yes we have a few. Come this way.'

She showed Kira a magnificent display of the most captivating flowers she'd ever seen. Beautifully sculptured, as though they'd been skilfully carved, they stood proud, their rainbow colours ranging from white, through pink, yellow and purple to the deepest blue.

' My grandson grows them,' Carrie said. 'There's nothing he doesn't know about orchids.'

Kira immediately fell in love with a white one, its flowers gracefully balanced on a long arching stem, like ballerinas dancing Swan Lake. 'Yes,' she said. 'This is the one.' Well, if she was going to take on a challenge she might as well make it a good one and one she'd enjoy.

'A good choice,' Carrie said. 'This should last a long time and give endless pleasure.'

Kira hummed to herself all the way home. She'd show Lisa how to grow orchids.

She set the orchid down and read the instructions on the label in the pot. It recommended a warm, humid, well-lit position, watered sparingly with spray misting in summer.

She placed it on the windowsill in the kitchen of the flat she shared with an old school friend's brother, Harry. Harry wasn't the best housemate in the world, but at least he kept himself to himself, usually out with his mates or spending long hours in his bedroom on the internet. Kira had the run of the place. The only times she saw him was in the mornings, scruffy in his pyjamas, usually recovering from a hangover. He wasn't the tidiest of people either, leaving unwashed cups and plates by the kitchen sink, but, for all his faults, Kira knew he meant well, and at least he paid his rent on time.

Every day she checked the orchid, did it need water, was the room warm enough, should she spray it again? Over the weeks she marvelled at the delicate blooms. One day she watched them dancing, dancing in the draught from the open window – open window! Her brow furrowed. Who opened the window? The kitchen was freezing.

'Harry,' she yelled. 'Did you open the window?'

Harry, staggered into the kitchen, rubbed the sleep from his eyes and brushed his hands through his unruly shock of hair. 'Oh yeah, I burnt the toast, had to get rid of the smoke.'

A week later the orchid's blossoms started to drop, its leaves turned brown. Kira was distraught. She lifted the pot out of its ceramic holder only to find her precious orchid had been sitting in water halfway up the pot. The earth it was planted in was sodden.

'Harry' , she yelled again.

'Oh, yeah,' he said. 'I watered it for you. It was dry as anything. I remembered how you always forgot to water your houseplants. Thought I was doing you a favour.'

Kira grimaced and went into town to get a replacement. She wasn't going to give up, but she didn't want to let Carrie know how quickly she'd managed to kill of the beautiful plant she'd bought from her. This time she put it on the coffee table in the lounge. A week later Harry knocked it off, spilling the earth and breaking the stem. The next replacement orchid lasted a whole month on the sill in her bedroom, before the petals fell and the leaves turned brown.

Kira sighed. Lisa's ability to keep her orchid alive for years was looking more and more awesome. But Kira wasn't going to give up. She'd go back and ask Carrie what she was doing wrong. Perhaps she could help.

As she walked into the florist she was surprised to see a man in a white shirt and jeans behind the counter. He was head-turningly handsome with intense blue eyes and shock of dark as night hair. Kira's heart fluttered like a schoolgirl on her first date when he smiled and asked her, 'How can I help you?'

Kira could think of a hundred ways he could help. Part of her was relieved not to have to explain to Carrie about the orchid. 'I want to buy an orchid,' she said.

'An orchid?' His eyes lit up sending shock waves through Kira. ' Fantastic,' he said. 'Orchids are magical. They signify love, luxury beauty and strength. Is it for a gift? Only they can convey a silent message, symbolising a special moment between you and your recipient.'

Kira's pulse quickened. 'Er, no,' she said. 'It's for me.'

'Oh,' he said. 'Most people buy them for gifts for people who don't have the faintest idea how to look after them. They're fragile flowers, but if treated properly they can last for years.'

'Really?' Kira said, noticing the way his eyes sparkled like sapphires when he talked about the plants. 'I guess you're some sort of expert then?'

'Some sort,' he said. He nodded to the certificates lining the wall. Kira glanced at them and it was clear he was more than 'some sort' of expert. He was the real thing. A prize winning orchid grower no less. 'I grow them for my Nan to sell here in the shop. I'm good at it too.'

'You must be Carrie's grandson. She told me about you.'

His gaze washed over her like a wave pulling her under. She knew instantly that she was done for. 'I wish she'd told me about you,' he said a wicked gleam in his eye. He held out his hand. 'I'm Adam by the way.'

Kira took his hand. It felt soft and warm and she wanted to cling on to it, but reluctantly let it go and explained about the disastrous history of her horticultural failures. 'I can't seem to grow anything but I did so want to have an orchid that didn't die on me. My sister's had an orchid for years,' she said. 'It's fabulous. Her husband bought if for her on their wedding day and she's kept ever since. Isn't that romantic?'

Adam frowned. 'Are you getting married then?' he asked. 'Is that why you want one?'

Kira gasped. 'No. No I've no plans in that direction, I just wanted to have an orchid like Lisa's.' Then she told him about the ones that had died and how her flatmate Harry had sabotaged all her efforts, and as she spoke tears welled up in her eyes.

Adam handed her a handkerchief. He seemed genuinely perturbed at her distress. 'If there's anything I can do,' he said. 'Perhaps I could help by keeping an orchid here for you, in the back room. It'd be your orchid but I'd look after it, nurture it and make sure it was all right. Would that help?'

Kira eyes widen. 'Would you? Would you do that for me? I wouldn't know how to thank you.'

His mega-watt smile could have lit a fire on an iceberg. 'You could have dinner with me tomorrow night. And you'd have to pop in every now and then to check on your orchid.'

Kira heart swelled. Two birds with one stone, she thought. Not only would she be able to have an orchid as lovely as Lisa's but she'd found the man of her dreams.

Six months later Kira was planning her wedding to Adam. Lisa was to be Matron of Honour. Kira went round to see her to discuss the dress she would wear. She pointed to Lisa's orchid, on the window sill, its arched stem still filled with a kaleidoscope of butterfly flowers.

'Adam's growing a special orchid for me for our wedding,' she said. 'I only hope I can keep it as long as you've kept yours.'

'What that one?' Lisa said nodding to the luxurious blooms in the window. 'I bought that last week.'

'Last week! But Ollie said it was the one he gave you on your wedding day.'

Lisa pouted. 'That died quite soon after,' she said, 'and I didn't want Ollie to get upset so I bought another one the same. In fact every time one dies I replace it. Ollie doesn't know.'

She stared at Kira. 'You won't tell Ollie will you? He'd be terribly hurt.'

(First published in Take a Break Fiction Feast in 2016)

May Your Wheels Always be Turning

"A cycling magazine?" Gary's eyes widened.

"Research," Petunia muttered, "for the article I'm writing."

The furrows on Gary's brow deepened. "But you don't know anything about cycling."

"I don't know anything about marathon running either, but it didn't stop me writing about that. It's called research. You can learn all you need to know on the internet without ever leaving your own front room."

Gary sighed. "That's just as well then, isn't it," he said and went to put the dinner on.

A couple of weeks later Petunia, face flushed with excitement, greeted him with a self-satisfied grin. "You remember that article I wrote about cycling? Well they've accepted it and asked me to write a monthly column. How about that?" She showed him the e-mail.

"Marcus Watson? Who's Marcus Watson?"

"Me. You wouldn't expect them to offer a monthly cycling column to someone called Petunia Shuttlebrick would you?"

Gary shook his head in bewilderment. "How can you write a monthly column about something you know nothing about, something you've never experienced, leastways, not since you were a teenager, what, thirty years ago?"

Petunia grimaced. Trust him to spoil everything – ever the wet blanket. He should be happy for her. Still, he did have a point. "That's the thing," she said. "They expect me to attend rallies and report on races; even take part in some of them."

"Well, that's it then. You can't can you?"

"No. But you could – as Marcus Watson."

"Me?"

"Yes. Why not? You're reasonably fit and you do have that old bike in the shed. You could go and tell me about it and I'll write is up. Perfect solution."

"You're mad." Gary turned to walk away.

"The money's amazing," she said.

He turned on his heel. "How amazing?"

A smile spread across his face when she told him. "I'll need to get into training," he said.

Gary retrieved his old racer from the shed, cleaned and oiled it, bought a new saddle and replaced the wheels.. Petunia watched as he swung his leg over the cross-bar. She'd never imagined him in Lycra before but found it quite exhilarating.

An hour later he returned, red faced and struggling for breath. "It's no good. I can't do it," he said. "Not at my age."

"Of course you can," Petunia insisted, rubbing his thigh. "You just need to get used to it. You can get used to anything in time."

Gary gazed at her. His face softened. He sighed and kissed her. "You win Pet," he said. A warm feeling flowed through her like melting butter. Best thing she ever did marrying Gary, he'd never let her down.

Over the following months Gary trained every night. He joined the local cycling club and faithfully reported to Petunia. He told her about the joy of feeling the wind in his face, the smell of the hedgerows as he sped along country roads, the freedom of free-wheeling down hills, the rallies and the races, the riders and their rivalries, the spats and petty jealousies; the cycling club proved to be a hot-bed of gossip and innuendo. "All grist to the mill," Petunia said. He took photos of the routes and riders and uploaded them on to Petunia's PC.

The column was a huge success. Petunia wrote it based on Gary's observations and anecdotes and passed it to him for his approval before sending it to the editor. If he made any comments she unfailingly accommodated his ideas. "We make a fantastic team," she said. "You do the research, I do the writing. Together we're invincible. I see a fabulous future ahead of us."

Gradually, his hair lightened in the sun, his face tanned and his body tightened. Fitter and more muscular he started watching his diet and gave up his nightly tipple. Instead of spending time in the pub at week-ends, he took long rides out into the country. A variety of cycling magazines arrived on Petunia's doorstep as Gary's passion for the sport grew. Petunia scanned them all for new markets for her writing.

One day, he suggested she include something about the helpers – the unsung heroes who turn out week after week in all weathers to provide refreshment, record times or work as marshals or stewards. "None of the rallies or races could go ahead without them," he said. "Their sterling efforts on our behalf should be recognised. There are some pictures on my iPhone."

While he showered Petunia scrolled through his phone looking for the photos. She checked his inbox. She froze as paralysing fear gripped her. A photo of Gary, grinning all over his stupid face, stared out at her. His arm was casually draped around the shoulders of a tall, good-looking, thirty-something blonde; her arm circled his waist, her head rested coyly on his now massive shoulders.

The message read '*You are the best. You brighten up my day. Looking forward to Sunday. Love xxx Mandy.*' She scrolled through several other texts, all light-hearted and flirty. All from Mandy. All with love and kisses.

A flush of hot blood rose through Petunia like the fire inside a volcano. Skinny as a straw and shallow as a saucer only half as interesting, she thought; just the sort to turn the head of a fast-approaching-mid-life-crisis man like Gary. An icy hand squeezed her heart. Tears sprang to her eyes.

"Who's Mandy?" she asked as casually as she could manage while they were dishing up the dinner.

"Mandy?"

"Yes – you brighten up my day, Mandy – remember?"

"Oh – Mandy? She's one of the helpers. Great girl. Very sporty."

I bet she is, Petunia thought, plonking an extra helping of potato on his plate.

Petunia was late getting the next edition of her column to the editor. So late in fact that she sent it without letting Gary see it. "Sorry, love," she said. "Deadline. You know how it is."

When the magazine arrived he turned to read her column. She watched the blood drain from his face his face as he read...

'It is with the deepest sadness and regret that we have learned of the tragic death of Marcus Watson, our cycling correspondent. Marcus was involved in a fatal accident at the foot of Hampton Hill when he skidded on ice into the path of an oncoming lorry. He was much loved within the cycling fraternity. He will be missed. His family have asked that his funeral be a private affair and we will respect their wishes. Anyone wishing to make a donation in his memory should send it to the Trauma Unit at the Royal Orthopaedic Hospital. RIP Marcus Watson, we were privileged to have known you. May your wheels always be turning. The Editor.

Gary raised his head to stare at her.

Petunia swung her wheelchair to face him. "I've got another project," she said, beaming with enthusiasm. "This one pays even better. It's about Formation Dancing for the Over Sixties. You'd be amazed how popular it is – there are groups and competitions and everything…"

(First published in The Weekly News in 2016)

Sunday's Child

Monday morning Jason pulled the dog-eared catalogue from his pocket and spread its pages across the bonnet of the car he was working on. Queasy with desire he wiped his hands down his overalls and studied the picture. A deep thrill ran through him. One more week and she would be his. He sighed, folded the paper and shoved it back into his pocket.

Tuesday he hurried into Motor Cycle City.

"Hi Jason, come to pick her up?" The salesman grinned. He'd seen Jason at the window every day for weeks gazing at the Harley Davidson Road King, his eyes bright with longing. He'd paid the deposit, the paperwork was ready. All he had to do now was sign the easy payments plan.

"Waste of money," Jason's dad said. "For that you could buy a decent car and have a holiday."

"Nah, cars and holidays are for old people," Jason said. His heart soared at the thought of the Harley.

Wednesdays, after work, Jason rode out with Tina, the other love of his life. Together they'd abandon themselves to the power of the machine beneath them and the heart-pumping adrenaline rush of exhilaration. They became as one, him, Tina and the Harley until, breathless, they'd stop in the hills, lie in the grass and stare at the stars. He loved Tina with all his heart, he really did.

A wet *Thursday* in July brought Jason's world crashing down.

"I'm pregnant," Tina said. "Up the spout, bun in the oven. I'm going to have your baby."

Jason glared at her. His throat constricted. He didn't want a baby - not now - probably not ever. They were too young – he wasn't ready. Of course he'd always planned to marry Tina – sometime in the future – the distant future - when he was ready to settle down, but right now he had a lot of living to do and his plans didn't include no baby. He felt the rest of his life slipping away.

"Don't look at me like that," she said. "I wasn't on my own up there in the hills was I?"

Things went rapidly downhill after that.

Friday nights, they went to the Black Jack Café, where rows of bikes glistened in the sun. All though the summer and into the autumn they'd roar off with the biker gang to meet up with other bikers swopping tales of road races, burn ups and bikes. This was living. This was what he was born for – not to spend his life trying to earn enough to support a family.

Families were for mugs. He preferred the freedom of the road.

"Soon be swopping your Harley for a pram," one of his mates said, "if what I hear is right."

Jason shook his head, his face set in grim determination. "Nah," he said. "No way – that ain't never gonna happen."

Saturday nights he would ride with Tina along the coast until they found somewhere to go clubbing until the early hours. But as time wore on and winter nights drew in Tina's waist expanded so she could no longer ride pillion. He couldn't face the ordeal of sitting with her parents; reproach filling their cold as the Arctic eyes, being reminded of his failings, so they'd walk to the pub.

Tina sat sipping her orange juice. "Of course it'll need a cot, bedding, nappies," she said. His eyes glazed over.

She gazed at him. "Do you think breast really is best?"

He shrugged and wished he was a thousand miles away. When she complained of backache and swollen ankles he said, "You need to put your feet up," and dropped her off early, riding out fast and far, lengthening the distance between them. Tina was no fun anymore. Gradually he stopped seeing her, preferring to spend his time with his biker mates.

One *Sunday* morning on a cold February day, he got the call. Tina was in hospital in labour. He hadn't seen her for months but hadn't managed to blot her out completely. Visions of her face, tears filling her eyes, niggled at the back of his mind.

He washed carefully, dressed and had his breakfast. Reluctance dragged his heels, a man on his way to his own hanging couldn't have been more downhearted. He had no interest in the baby – babies were smelly things that cramped your lifestyle. Babies were things for women to ogle at. He wished with all his might he could jump on his Harley and ride into the sunset, but it was a distant dream. He owed it to Tina to go to the hospital – he knew that.

A nurse showed him to Tina's room. Tina radiated happiness. She glowed. The smile on her face reached the sky. She held a bundle in her arms. Jason swallowed – this was it – the moment he'd dreaded. Tina held the bundle out to him. He laid the flowers he'd bought on the bed. She placed the infant in his arms.

"Meet your daughter," she said.

Holding her in his arms his heart squeezed. A maelstrom of emotions swept over him. His stomach knotted and his preconceptions melted like butter. He stared mesmerized at her scarlet, puckered face, a miniature of his own. Entranced, he touched her tiny fingers. She snuffled and moved. His heart raced, his defences crumbled. A huge swell of love rose up in him. He saw the child she would become and the lifetime stretching ahead of her.

Tears filled his eyes, a lump rose in his throat. "Don't worry Pet," he said. "I'll be here to look out for you." As he said it he knew it to be true.

"I'm thinking of calling her Hailey. Sounds like the bike," Tina said.

His head shot up. "The Harley?" He gazed at the baby sleeping in his arms. "I'll have to sell that now won't I?" He grinned. "Can't take a nipper out on the back of a motorbike can we?"

KAY SEELEY

My Wild Irish Rover

I'll never forget the first summer I spent with my great aunt Clara. I was seventeen, she was about seventy and County Wexford in Ireland was the last place on earth that I wanted to be.

Great Aunt Clara lost her husband to a heart attack the year I was born. I'm not sure whether my being named after her was supposed to be some sort of consolation, or whether there was more to it than that. Everyone said she'd 'married well' when she married Paddy, an irrepressible Irish entrepreneur said to have found gold at the end of his particular rainbow.

"He may be a Wild Irish Rover," my grandmother said, "but she'll want for nowt."

Dad had wanted to name me Lily after his mother but Mum said his family hadn't two ha'pennies to rub together. She insisted on calling me Clara after my wealthy, recently bereaved, childless great aunt.

I grew up overshadowed by my namesake. I hardly knew her, but grew up intimidated by her reputation. Mum said she could haggle for Ireland and win. "Nobody puts anything over on Aunt

Clara," she said. "Sharp as a tack, she is. You'd do well to follow her example."

I remember her visiting when I was about five. I was rolled out for her approval.

"Not much to her," she'd said looking me up and down. "A sorry looking bag of bones if you ask me. Still, she's time to grow I suppose."

Mum and Dad treated her like royalty and when I finished school my mother insisted I spend the summer visiting my namesake in Ireland.

"She's an old lady and you can make yourself useful," Mum said. "Won't do any harm to get to know her. She's family after all."

"Aye and she's got money than God," my grandmother said with a sly grin.

It wasn't my idea of fun. I was just out of school and filled with the arrogant confidence of any teenager waiting to go to Uni. A far as I was concerned Great Aunt Clara had nothing to offer that could possibly compare to the thrill of a gap year backpacking around the world, but Mum was adamant. I thought perhaps if I made the effort I could make some excuse after a couple of days and catch up with my friends.

The cottage where Great Aunt Clara lived was a short walk from the fishing village of Kilmore Quay. The stone walled cottage was huge and rambling. Rambling? I should have said crumbling, it's grandeur obscured by an overgrown jungle of vegetation. Large chunks of thatch hung from the roof leaving gaping holes to let in the rain, the white-washed walls were blackened and peeling. In picture-postcard order the place would have appeared imposing but it had clearly fallen into disrepair. It now carried the look of faded gentility, I saw no sign of the great wealth and enviable lifestyle Mum always attributed to Great Aunt Clara.

Unsure that I was in the right place I timidly lifted the brass knocker on the multi-stained, oak door and announced my presence with several loud raps. I heard shuffling feet and then my great aunt appeared, shorter than I remembered and more rounded. Her auburn hair had faded and was streaked with gold. Her clothes were fresh and bright but dated. Tan leather sandals encased her well worn feet. Eyes sharp as emerald chips appraised me. I shuddered beneath her scrutiny. Even at her age she remained a formidable woman.

"So, you're Clara," she said. "Well, you'd better come in."

She stood aside to let me pass into the hall. A quick glance at the browning wallpaper told me the inside was as poorly maintained as the outside.

"Upstairs, turn left, first door on your right. I'll leave you to get settled," she said. "You'll excuse my not coming up. I've got a jam pan bubbling on the stove. Don't want it to burn."

'Not the warmest welcome in the world,' I thought. She wasn't at all what I'd expected.

"Thanks," I said, managing to control the frisson of alarm that ran through me. What on earth had I let myself in for? And what had happened to my great aunt's supposed riches?

Upstairs I unpacked my few possessions into a rickety chest of drawers and even more rickety wardrobe. The room was surprisingly pleasant. Sunlight poured in through sparkling windows, the walls were freshly painted in pale pastels and the rainbow quilt covering the bed matched the cheerful curtains. Bunches of dried lavender scented the air. I smiled. My great aunt had gone to a great deal of trouble to ensure my comfort, despite her off-hand welcome.

Heartened, I ventured downstairs to find her in the kitchen scooping jam into sparkling jars. I watched as she put rings of waxed paper on top of the jam and sealed the jars with covers dipped in cold water and stretched over the top to be held in place by elastic bands. Once the jam was finished she and took two glasses from a cupboard and a jug of lemonade from an ancient fridge. "We can take this outside," she said handing me a glass, "then I'll show you around."

She led me outside onto the terrace where a table and several wrought iron chairs sat in the shade of the huge climbing roses covering the overhead beams. The air was filled with their scent, an aroma I came to associate with great aunt Clara. Beyond that the garden stretched as far as I could see. A sizeable plot near to house had been cultivated to provide a kitchen garden full of vegetables, soft fruit, herbs. Further on, in the middle of a rough, overgrown patch of grassland and tangled bushes I saw an archway, so dense with brambles it veiled the pond that lay along its length. Behind that I could just make out a substantial orchard.

"Your mother tells me you're eager to help out," Clara said. "Not that I haven't been managing for years. Still, another pair of hands wouldn't go amiss I suppose."

I felt a cold thud in my heart as I realised I'd been sent to ingratiate myself to this redoubtable woman by working in the house and garden that time forgot. There was no sign of the lavish lifestyle my mother had predicted.

Later, over a supper of fresh caught mackerel and vegetables from the garden Aunt Clara said, "Not what you expected is it?"

I shrugged. "I'm not sure what I expected," I said, untruthfully. "I thought it might be a bit less – a bit more – I mean – well, more…" I was lost for words.

Aunt Clara chuckled. "Never believe all you hear," she said. "Appearances can be deceptive. That's something your mother never understood." She took a sip of last year's Elderberry wine. "How is she? Your mother? Still trying to keep up with the Joneses?"

I grinned. "Actually I think she's trying to overtake them," I said.

Clara's whole face lit up and her eyes sparkled like diamonds when she laughed. "You'll do," she said.

Over the weeks I gradually got to know Aunt Clara. Old fashioned and slightly faded she reminded me of a well worn sofa, bulging in odd places, sometimes uncomfortable but always reliable. Our days fell into a rhythm of breakfast, working in the garden, lunch, then either a stroll along to the harbour to visit the small shops and buy fish for our tea, or along the cliffs where Clara, resplendent in a sunflower patterned shawl and huge red straw hat tied on with a pale blue chiffon scarf, would set up her easel to paint. Then I would wander along the beach to sunbathe, swim or feast on fresh strawberries and cream until tea-time.

Sometimes I'd walk to the harbour to buy ice cream. That's where I met Erik, a Norwegian student working on the boats for the season. I'd just bought a triple scoop cornet and turned to walk back along the quay when this man-mountain roller-skated into me. Luckily he managed to catch me in his arms, spinning me around to prevent us both falling to the ground. Most of my ice-cream ended up on the floor, apart from the bits that were smeared down his shirt. He was unlike anyone I'd ever met before. A hearty zest for life shone in his cornflower blue eyes.

"I'm sorry," we chorused in unison. Then we both laughed.

"I'm so sorry, it was my fault," he said in his clipped English. I was immediately smitten. He smiled and the day suddenly became brighter. He insisted on buying me another ice-cream and escorting me to a seat by the harbour so I could enjoy it in safety. That was the beginning of a magical summer. I still remember his crazy sense of humour, the hesitation and precision in his voice when he spoke and the way my heart soared at his easy laughter. Tall, broad-shouldered and blonde, Clara called him 'my catch of the day'. Those glorious summer days and cloudless skies had a rich mellowness only ever recalled in retrospect.

Erik was studying Marine Biology. He opened my eyes to the beauty beneath the sea and the wonders of nature all around us. He told me about the rock formations and the cycles of the moon and how they affected the tides. Our summer romance was brief but it changed my life. He'd awakened within me a thirst for learning. When I returned home I switched my course to study the things that Erik studied.

I was surprised Clara did everything herself.

"I used to help my father on the allotment," she told me one evening after supper. "Soon as I was old enough to hold a trowel," she said. She smiled and stared at the sky as she recalled her childhood. "We didn't have much in those days, but then nobody did." She sighed. "We helped each other out. If we had anything to spare we'd share it with our neighbours and they with us." She paused. "Not like today," she added. I caught a hint of bitterness in her voice.

One lunch-time we were sitting out on the terrace when I saw some boys creeping among the apples trees in the orchard. I pointed them out to Clara. "Should I chase them away?" I said.

She chuckled. "Heavens no," she said. "I have more than I need. If they asked I'd give them the apples but they prefer scrumping – it gives them a feeling of doing something naughty, something forbidden. That makes it exciting. We should all have some excitement in our lives when we are young." She stopped to gaze down the garden for a few minutes. "You can shout at them now if you like. It'll give them a shock and make it even more thrilling."

So I did.

It was just as Clara had predicted. Whooping and yelling they made a frenzied exit over the fence carrying their haul of illicit fruit. I could hear their howls of delight all the way along the lane.

Another time I asked her why she didn't get someone in to clear the garden and cut back the brambles that covered the archway over the pond in impenetrable profusion.

"What, and frighten the dragonflies," she said. "I prefer dragonflies to people – they have no sense of status. They swoop and chase in their iridescent colours and bring nothing but good cheer. Why would I want to disturb them, they've done nothing to harm me?" She smiled wryly. "I did have a gardener once but he died and I have never felt the need to replace him."

Once a week Clara would take a basket of fruit and veg from the garden to the ramshackle fishing sheds by the harbour, where colourful boats rocked gently on the waves and the air became salty with sea breezes and the pervasive smell of fish. She'd stop and chat to the woman who sorted the fish and mended the nets and pots.

"Marie's got six kids to feed," she told me, "and her husband lost at sea." She'd leave the fruit and vegetables, together with some eggs, cheese or ham she'd bought in the market.

"There's too much for me," she'd say, "and Clara here doesn't eat much." One day Marie offered Aunt Clara a fresh lobster but Aunt Clara refused it. "I could never bring myself to cook it," she said with a grimace. "Not while it's alive."

That evening she told me about moving to Ireland and how she missed her family. "We were close, your grandmother and me. Being the youngest and only girls with six brothers we stuck up for one another. We shared everything, clothes, make up, hair clips." Clara eyes clouded over. "I did miss her when I got married. This time of year I'd always think of her and how, when we were kids, we'd go Blackberrying together and our Mum, your great grandma, would make jam. Sugar was on ration then so she'd swap eggs from the chickens your great granddad kept for the sugar. It was like that in those days, everyone helping everyone else out."

Gradually I came to understand my great aunt. She hated waste. I guessed it was a legacy of her upbringing. Everything she had was used. Heads of the fish were given to a neighbour for her cat, peelings and left-over food was used for compost or taken to the pig farm. She would shake her head at the antics of the kids today, saying they had things too easy. I suppose, compared to her generation, we did.

I once asked her why she didn't get people in to help around the house and garden, given that she was reputed to be quite wealthy. She laughed.

"Would that make for a better life do you think?" She said, leaning on the fork she was using to dig the potatoes. "Would my life be any better or more fulfilled if I had people in to do everything for me?" A look of determination crossed her face. "I have everything I need. I do as I please. I am quite content. The happiest people I know have very little. Anyway, Aiden from the garage helps from time to time with the heavy digging in return for some of the produce to take home to his mam."

I thought of my mother and her endless aspirations. That summer taught me what was important in life.

I went back to visit Clara the following year, and the year after that, then I decided to stay. I'd met my own Wild Irish Rover. His name was Finn and he was a fisherman. His hair was black as night and his eyes the colour of a summer sky. I was nineteen by then and I'd grown weary of the lads at home and their broken promises. Finn offered nothing, promised nothing but gave me everything. The laughter dancing in his eye, his simple philosophy of life and the way he made me feel all came free. We met on the Quay where he was unloading one of the boats. At first glance he was just one of the boys but he had a vitality about him that didn't diminish as he chatted, flirted outrageously and gently teased me. I was instantly and instinctively drawn to him. His boyish charm and soft Irish lilt made my heart scramble and flounder. He had a mischievous sense of fun, humour that folded me in half with laughter and a capacity for kindness that left me gasping.

On our first date he took me to a ceili dance. Clara assured me that the music would be lively and the craic legendary. She wasn't wrong. We'd hardly arrived before the hall exploded into life as the band struck up. Within minutes the floor heaved with dancers, reeling, skipping and yoo-hooing to the rhythm of the music. Finn pulled me onto the floor into a line of whirling dancers spinning so fast I could hardly catch my breath. It was impossible not to be swept up in the excitement. The swirling colours the rousing voice of the caller, the pounding of feet and the clapping along with the energy of the music. At the end of the evening, breathless but eyes sparkling, I felt a stab of disappointment that it was almost over.

When Finn took me in his arms for the last waltz he set my heart on fire. I danced with my cheek pressed to his face, feeling the slight stubble on his chin and breathing in his woody aroma. I had to suppress a smile when I realised I'd expected him to smell of fish. I knew then that I wasn't going home, that this was where I belonged, that we'd be together forever.

My biggest regret is that Clara didn't live to see us wed. She died just before the wedding, but not before I'd asked her about her alleged 'great wealth'.

She chuckled. "Paddy was a gambler," she said, "he took huge risks just for the thrill of it. Our fortunes went up and down quicker than a frog flicking flies." Her face spread into a smile. "Oh, the excitements of it – we travelled the world you know, stayed in the best hotels, saw everything. I wouldn't have missed it for a bucket of gold. When we were up we soared so high we could touch the stars and even when we were down Paddy had a way with him and we were never down for long. After he'd gone I found out we'd lost everything except the house. He never risked that."

She looked at me. "People treat you differently when they think you have money" she said. "We fooled 'em didn't we?"

I thought of my parents and the way they fawned over her. I squeezed her hand. "You sure did," I said with a grin. Her fabulous wealth, so beloved by my mother, was an illusion. Her riches lay in the people she knew, the friends she made and the life she lived. My memories of Clara are more precious than jewels.

She left me and Finn the cottage and the grounds. We'll move in when it's been renovated and the garden put back into some sort of shape. Should be ready by the time the baby's due. If it's a girl we're going to call her Clara.

(First published in Woman's Weekly Fiction special in 2014)

A Helping Hand

Things don't always go according to plan do they? Mark thought as he stood outside his uncle's house. Ten years ago, when he'd left he'd vowed never to return, yet, here he was back again. He sighed, picked up his bags and let himself into the house.

Inside, the warmth embraced him, fond memories flooded his brain, but not all his memories of Huddleswick were as pleasant.

He left his bags in the hall and went to see his uncle. Uncle Bill had been like a father to him after his parents died. He'd been seven then and destined to go into what they euphemistically called 'care'. This florid faced, affable man had taken him in, fed him, clothed him, supported him, made sure he did his homework and stood on the touchlines shouting encouragement at his feeble attempts to play sports. He'd sat with him for hours dealing with his schoolboy angst, building his confidence and willing him on through the heartaches of his teenage years. He'd been as overjoyed as Mark when he gained a place at Oxford. Some debts can never be repaid, he thought.

His heart faltered when he saw how frail the old man looked. He'd aged, but then, Mark reasoned, he'd been ill. He forced a smile and reassurance into

47

his voice. "How are you doing, you old devil?" he said.

Bill took Mark's hand, holding it fast in his. "Good to see you back," he said. "I wish you could stay."

Mark saw a world of longing in the old man's face, his eyes wet with hope. Guilt washed over him but he managed to shake it off. He'd taken two months leave from the solicitors' office in London where he worked to help out at his uncle's estate agency; he had no intention of moving back to Yorkshire.

"Take more than a heart attack to kill off an old goat like you," he said. "You'll be right as rain in a couple of weeks."

On Monday morning Mark's first appointment was to view a cottage on Halleywell Hill. Buried behind surrounding trees at the end of a muddy lane it appeared isolated and inaccessible. The property consisted of side-by-side farm dwellings, two-up and two-down, which had been knocked into one to produce a larger family home.

"You have to see the granddaughter," his uncle told him. "She's arranging the sale. Wants to move Granny into a Home or some such. The old lady's in her eighties, so be polite."

"I'm always polite," Mark said with a grin, "especially to old ladies."

The drive up the hill past his old school brought back a deluge of childhood memories, all bad. A skinny lad he'd been teased unmercifully by the bigger boys. With no Mum and Dad to look out for him he was fair game. They laughed at him in his old fashioned clothes and his head always in a book. They called him 'worm' and stole his pocket money. They beat him up and took his homework to pass off as their own. His Uncle Bill hugged him, showered him with affection and tried to teach him not to care, but the hurt couldn't be brushed away as easily as his tears. His jaw hardened at the memory.

A sprightly old lady with grey hair and twinkling eyes opened the door for him. He checked his notes. "Mrs Holmes? I'm from Morley's, the estate agent"

"You'll be wanting to see Stella," she said. "You'd best come in."

Inside the cottage was bright and welcoming. Mark took in the polished brasses, the log fire burning in the grate, the cosy feel of the room. A loving home, he thought gazing around, and felt a tightening in his chest. The obvious warmth and comfort inside the cottage was completely at odds with his recollection of the hostile coldness of the world outside.

"Stella won't be long, I'll put the kettle on."

Mark heard a car draw up outside and then Stella burst into the room. His heart clenched. Stella Robinson stood before him, not the Stella Robinson he remembered from school, but a grown up, fully matured, gorgeous, flame-haired Stella Robinson, with fire dancing in eyes that sparkled like emeralds. He swallowed.

"Ah," she said. "The Estate Agent. You're a lot younger than I expected, but never mind. Let's get started." Her voice was strident, urgent, rushed. She's in a hurry, he thought, but then, he recalled, she always was.

Mark tried to still his trembling hands. He flicked through his paperwork to catch his breath. She didn't remember him, but he remembered her. A big girl, larger-than-life loud, bossy even then, but she'd been nice to him. He'd almost died of embarrassment when, like a fire-cracker, she'd stood up against the bigger boys, shaming them into giving him back his dinner-money. He'd had a crush, admired her from a distance but never had the courage to approach. She'd been ambitious and destined to fly high. She was still beautiful: glossy hair, peach skin, immaculately groomed; he couldn't take his eyes off her. She always was too good for Huddleswick and as out of reach as the stars in the heavens above.

"I'll show the young man around," the old lady said carrying in a tray of tea and cakes. "Give you a chance to take your coat off and settle." She put the tray on the coffee table in front of the fire. "Now, come along young man," she said. "You must call me Elsie."

Mark followed her up the stairs. Every room they went into was light and trim. Every bed had a different coloured patchwork quilt with matching curtains, the assorted wooden bedside and dressing tables were a little scarred with wear, but highly polished, the windows shone, the mirrors gleamed, pots of lavender and lemon scented the rooms. "This is quite charming," he said. "You obviously care a great deal about your home."

"I do," Elsie said.

Mark gazed out of the window. He noticed the overgrown hedges the long grass, the untidy, unkempt paths. The garden, flush with full blown roses, sloped down to a line of Willows edging a small stream. Beyond that the hills rose in sheep spotted fields bordered by trees, clothed in autumn glory, to the far horizon. The peace and tranquillity of the scene stirred feelings inside him he hadn't had for some time: feelings of gratitude and contentment. "If I had a view like this, I'd want to stay here forever," he said.

"I do," Elsie whispered. She sighed and turned away. "It's all too much for me you see, especially the garden. My husband was the gardener, God rest him. Stella wants me to move nearer to her, so she can keep an eye on me." She turned to Mark, watery tears in her eyes. "I had a fall you see. Not safe to be left on my own Stella says." She shook her head sadly. "She's probably right, she usually is." She sighed and moved unsteadily towards the door, her shoulders sagging.

Mark turned, his gaze drawn once more to the view. He wanted to snatch it, keep it safe forever pressed into memory, a moment of serenity in a mad, mad world.

Downstairs Stella was waiting. "Well, what do you think? When can you put it on the market? We need to move quickly. There's a vacancy at a

Retirement Home near me in Leeds, but it won't be there for long."

Mark grimaced. Super-efficient as ever, he thought, always in a rush. "I've made some notes. I'll take them back to the office and come up with some figures." He stood and shook Stella's hand; the brief contact sent shock waves racing through his body. "I'll be in touch," he said.

Driving away from the cottage he mused, Stella Robinson? Who'd have thought?

His next call was on a young couple living on the ninth floor of a tower block. Riding up in the urine soaked lift he shuddered. It was a world away from the cottage and the old lady. Gritty reality, he thought. This is where I could have ended up if it hadn't been for Uncle Bill.

The young man who greeted him wore jeans and a check work-shirt. His hands were large, red and calloused; shaking them brought home to Mark how smooth and slender his own were. The young man's wife, a slip of a thing in her early twenties, was similarly dressed in jeans, her blonde hair pulled back into an elastic band. Pale with dark shadows beneath her eyes, she looked as though she hadn't slept for a week, which Mark thought probably was the case when he saw the infant in the Moses basket in the lounge.

"We're looking for somewhere to rent," the husband, Richard, according to Mark's papers, said.

"Preferably on the ground floor," his wife chipped in.

"We'd like a garden," Richard added, "but that's probably out of our price range." He smiled and squeezed his wife's hand. "I'm in regular work with lots of overtime and we'd really like an extra room for the baby if possible."

Mark looked through the rental application, calculated an affordable rent and said "I'll see what I can do. Of course, prices around here are quite prohibitive..."

The husband and wife looked alarmed.

"Don't worry, I'll do the best I can for you," Mark said and at that moment realised that he meant it. He'd go back to his uncle and find the best deal he could for them, even if it meant haggling with landlords. Driving back he sighed. Going soft in your old age, he thought and chuckled.

By the end of the week working with his uncle Mark saw the agency in a different light. He'd been reluctant to commit to more than a month helping out, but now he saw endless possibilities.

"I've no one else," his uncle said with a gleam in his eye. "When I'm gone this will all be yours."

"Not for a while yet, I hope," Mark said.

As a solicitor he thought he'd seen the worst of people, picking up the pieces of their lives, sorting out their difficulties and disputes attempting to find solutions to insoluble problems, but now, working as an estate agent he saw his problem solving abilities differently; he could actually change people's lives.

Later that week he went to see Elsie, knowing Stella wouldn't be there. Over tea and cakes they chatted. Elsie talked about Stella's meteoric rise in the business world and her inability to sustain a personal relationship for more than a couple of months. "She's not an easy person," she said, "but she has a heart of gold."

"You don't want to leave here do you?" he said.

Elsie bowed her head. "I'm sure Stella knows what's best," she said sadly.

Mark's voice softened. "If you restored the house to the original two cottages you could live in one and let the other. The rent would cover the cost and the tenants could do the garden and keep an eye on you," he said.

Elsie's face lit up as though all her Christmases had come at once. "What a wonderful idea." She paused, looking doubtful. "Do you think you could…?"

"What? Make the arrangements? Sure." He had the perfect tenants in mind.

"No, not that, although that would be great." She twisted her hands anxiously. "No, could you explain it to Stella, you know, persuade her?" Her eyebrows rose in hope.

Mark chuckled. Stella wasn't that scary, he thought, and he loved a challenge. Visions of telling her over a candlelit supper sprang to mind. "My pleasure," he said.

Driving back, his heart was full of optimism. Perhaps Huddleswick wasn't such a bad place to live after all he thought.

(First published in Woman's Weekly Fiction Special in 2013)

The Man Who Painted Trees

I used to love trees. I loved the whispering of their leaves and the way they swayed in the wind. I loved sitting in their shade in summer, their exotic blooms and wonderful smells. I loved the starkness of their bare branches against an opalescent sky in winter, the way raindrops hung shimmering and snow lay white against the darkness. I loved the rich, golden tapestry of autumn and the hopeful buds of spring. That was before I met Peter.

Peter was an artist, he painted trees.

I was a student working a summer job waiting tables in my brother's café in the park. It was always hectic with families coming in for coffee while their offspring fed the ducks or played on the swings. The park was a hub of activity with children whooping and running in the sunshine, ball games, bicycles, noise and laughter.

I noticed Peter the first time he came in. Head-turningly handsome his sandy hair was tousled, his jeans paint spattered. A rucksack was slung carelessly over one shoulder and an easel hung over the other. The women milling around the cake display case, barred his way. I watched him edge awkwardly around them. He waited patiently while the children in front of him chose their treats, first this one, then that one. They could never make up their minds. He smiled and caught my eye. I smiled too and somehow the day seemed brighter. I think I knew then that there was something special about him. He had an easy charm and a winning smile.

He ordered a coffee to go, then scanned the pastries in the cabinet on the counter. "And a Danish," she said with a grin.

I served him then watched him stroll to a spot by the lake where he set up his easel. It would be the perfect place to paint the weeping willow dipping its fronds into cool water, as long as he didn't mind the children throwing bread to the ducks all around him.

He came back in the afternoon, but I was busy waiting on tables. He stood watching for while, then waved goodbye as he went.

The next morning he came in for his coffee. "And a Danish?" I asked.

He grinned. "Why not?" he said.

Later that day I saw him by the cricket pitch. He sat a little way away from the line of Poplars that shaded the Pavilion. On the third day he was by the cycle track where a Larch stood proudly on a small hill. I strolled over. I was captivated by his long slender fingers plying the brush that brought life to the image on the page.

He turned to look at me. A wide spontaneous smile lit up his face. A thrill ran down my spine. "You're very good," I said. "Do you mind me watching?"

A twinkle of mirth danced in eyes that sparkled like sunlight on water. "I've watched you waiting on tables so I guess it's only fair if you watch me," he said.

I laughed. "It's not quite the same is it?" I said. "I don't want to disturb you if it puts you off."

He chuckled. "You won't put me off," he said. My pulses raced.

That was the beginning. Every day I found myself drawn to him, eager to find out where he was working, eager to see him again. Whenever I found him my heart lifted a little.

"Why only paint the trees?" I asked when I noticed the tree standing alone on the page.

"People like trees," he said. "They look good on the wall. There's tranquillity and a sense of purpose with a tree. Each tree is different – like people trees have different personalities."

I gazed at the Lebanese Cedar he was painting. It was my favourite tree in the park. I tried to see its sense of purpose and its personality but it escaped me. "Okay," I said. "Tell me about the personality of the cedar."

He stopped painting, put his brushes down and glanced at me. His gazed washed over me like a wave, pulling me under. My heart stumbled. He rose and stood beside me. I felt the warmth of his presence and the world tilted.

"Look at the cedar," he said, "and tell me what you see."

"I see a tree."

He sighed. "Look how tall the cedar stands. Its branches spread across it like clouds. It's a sturdy, serious tree. Even a strong wind hardly ruffles its branches. It's enduring, coniferous and unchanging. Its roots are deep. It's like a kindly grandfather, silent and wise spreading its branches to shelter those who sit beneath it."

I held my breath. His passion was obvious. He saw it through artist's eyes. All I saw was a tree.

"Don't all trees do that?" I asked innocently.

He laughed and shook his head. "Think of the willow. It bends in the wind. It's a secret, whispering tree. You can hide in the embrace of its dipping fronds but it's fickle. If the wind blows it lifts its arms and you will be discovered. Never trust a willow, it bends whichever way the wind blows."

I was beginning to see what he meant by the trees' differing personalities. I even imagined the willow blowing in the wind. "All right," I said. "What about the oak?"

He gathered up his things and packed away his easel. He gazed at me again, a speculative gaze as though studying my intent. "If you're really interested, meet me by the oak tomorrow," he said, hoisting his rucksack onto his back as he walked away. "Bring coffee," he called over his shoulder.

The next day I learned that the oak was majestic but full of its own importance. Its size gave it charisma other trees lacked. It symbolised strength and power but also patience, perseverance and hard work.

Over the weeks he explained the virtues of the trees: the elder, which Peter said was feminine, wise and bountiful in its nature, the Birch; a symbol of new beginnings and the Ash with its healing properties. His voice warmed and he came alive as he talked about the Larch, which is said to ward off evil spirits and prevent enchantment. Unfortunately it didn't prevent me being enchanted by Peter. I was smitten.

"Who buys the paintings?" I asked one day.

"People tend to buy the pictures of trees that most reflect themselves," he said. "I can usually tell when I meet them which pictures they will buy." He paused as if unsure then said, "I've an exhibition at a local gallery if you're interested. I could take you tonight."

Of course I had to go with him. It was amazing seeing his pictures on the white gallery walls. I saw what he meant about the people too. Every time a buyer was interested in a picture Peter told them about the personality of the tree and its history. A bear of a man dressed in tweed bought the oak, a thin, wiry, red-headed man bought the copper beech and a tall, middle-aged man in a suit bought the Larch which he said was for his daughter.

A tall spiky woman dressed in purple showed a lot of interest in the picture of a May tree in full blossom. It was beautiful.

"You have to watch out for the May," Peter said. "Its blossoms hide thorns. Myths and legends surround it, making it dark and mystical. Cutting its branches and bringing them indoors is said to bring bad luck. Its flowers carry the smell of death."

"I'll take it," the woman said. "It sounds right up my street."

We laughed, but even then I saw Peter had a way with him. He was sensitive, intelligent and totally irresistible.

Every day, after I'd finished my shift in the café, I'd wander over to wherever he was painting. Then he'd pack his things and we'd spend the evening together. I'll never forget the first time he kissed me. We'd gone to a club. The music was blaring, the air stuffy with heat and the sweat of a multitude of dancers. Neon lights flashed all around us. He casually put his arm around my waist and pulled me towards him. Fireworks exploded inside me as I melted into his arms. If I live to be a hundred no kiss would ever be as sweet.

I felt close to him, closer than I'd ever felt to anybody; the sort of closeness that brings a special kind of intimacy. I'm sure the scientists have a name for it but I just thought of it as magic moments when we could be together and forget the rest of the world.

All that summer I was lunatic with love. I remember endless galleries, late night chips in steamy cafes, balmy summer evenings watching him paint, or if it was too wet, long walks in the rain when we'd stand by the lake looking for the rainbow.

He gave me a painting of the Cedar, the one I had admired so much.

"The most stunning tree for the most stunning girl," he said. But there was something elusive about him. Something I couldn't quite pin down.

I hung the painting on the wall in the café so I could see it every day.

Towards the end of that summer, the leaves on the trees turning golden in the sun, he told me he was moving on. I looked into his eyes, shining with tenderness, and asked him why.

"It's time," he said. My heart crumbled like the dried up dying leaves.

I sighed and glanced around, biting my lip to stop from crying. "Will you come back?"

"I might," he said. "Who knows?"

As the leaves on the trees fell that autumn my tears fell with them but I knew I had to let him go.

Autumn's chill blew through the park, rustling the remaining leaves. The skies clouded over and that 'end of summer' feeling shadowed my heart. The café closed up for the winter. I was going on to uni, a fresh start and a new beginning. Not a day went by I didn't think of him, his summer blue eyes, tousled hair and magical smile. Each summer I wondered if he'd return. He never did.

I thought I would forget him, but I never have. I've moved on of course, met my husband George and got married. We have children who fill my life with joy and happiness, but they say you never forget your first love.

I look at the trees now and my heart aches. He was a free spirit who couldn't be tied down, blown this way and that like the willow; I was the deep-rooted cedar, solid reliable and strong, but unmoving. What we shared was fleeting, like long summer days, and the more precious for being so. I still have the picture of the Lebanese Cedar hanging on my wall. I look at it now and then with fond memories of what might have been. I can't regret the past, but I look at the trees with different eyes now; trees that held him more completely than I ever could.

(First published in People's Friend Magazine in 2016)

Forever Friends

'I'm surprised you let her play with that girl from the Estate,' I heard Auntie Sarah say to Mum over afternoon tea in the garden. Of course I wasn't supposed to be listening but she was talking about my best friend Marcie, so not being supposed to hear only made it more interesting.

She sipped her tea and said, 'They're like two peas in a pod. I'm surprised no one has said anything. Same seeds, different gardens.'

I couldn't think what she meant. She also said something about jeans. I'm not allowed to wear jeans but Marcie wears them all the time.

I've been best friends with Marcie ever since she started at my school. She's a year younger than me but as soon as we met in the playground we sort of clicked and we've been forever friends ever since. I don't care that she lives on the Estate and I never knew Auntie Sarah was such a snob.

When I saw posters for the Fair that was coming to town for the Bank Holiday I couldn't wait to go. I'd never been to the fair. Dad always takes us away in August but we were home this year. Excitement bubbled up inside me. I asked Mum if we could go.

'Dad's taking us to the Science Museum,' she said. 'Afterwards we can all go to McDonald's. Won't that be fun?'

Not as much fun as going to the fair I thought. My heart sank to my boots. 'I'd rather go to the fair,' I said. 'Everyone I know is going to the fair. Even Auntie Sarah is going.' Hope lit up my heart. 'I could go with Marcie,' I said.

Mum cradled my face in her hands. 'The fair's not for you sweetheart,' she said. She had a faraway look in her eyes when she said it.

A week later we were back at school. I didn't really mind. It was good to see my old friends again. Everyone had been to the fair except me. They couldn't stop talking about it.

As part of our PSHE lesson we learnt about how babies are made. I found the bit about 'seeds' and genes most interesting. Genes not jeans. I remembered what Auntie Sarah had said about me and Marcie. That's ridiculous, I thought. How can Marcie and me be 'same seeds' and have the same genes? I guess we do look a bit alike. We've both got blue eyes, but Marcie's tumble of jet-black curls touch her shoulders, whereas Mum keeps my ebony locks short. Marcie's had gold rings in her ears since she was three. Mum wouldn't let me get my ears pierced. We both have birthdays in May. I wanted to have a joint party but Dad said no. Sometimes I think he's like Auntie Sarah and disapproves of Marcie. I heard her tell Mum she'd have to curb my wayward ways or I'd grow wild. Marcie's always getting into scrapes.

Marcie lives on the Estate and has five brothers. I live in The Avenue and have only one. My dad's a solicitor, Marcie doesn't have a dad unless...

I got a bad feeling thinking about it, like a stone lodged under my ribs making it difficult to breathe. I felt sick, but still...I couldn't get Auntie Sarah's words out of my mind. 'Same seeds' what did she mean?

That night at dinner I swallowed and asked Dad if he knew Marcie's mum and did he like her?

He looked shocked. He ran his fingers through his sandy hair, hummed and hawed a bit and then said, 'I don't know her well enough to form an opinion.' His face flushed, but that could have been irritation. I've noticed he resembles a beetroot when he gets into a paddy.

'But do you think she's pretty?' I persisted.

He huffed again. 'Not as pretty as you poppet,' he said, moving around the table to kiss my head. 'Now finish your dinner and get on with your homework,' so that was the end of that conversation.

The next day over the park I thought I'd ask Marcie about you know what. She's younger than me but knows a lot more about that sort of thing. It was getting late and I had to get home soon. Dusk was falling, the amber lights from the nearby street cast long shadows over the swings where we were sitting.

I took a breath. 'Do you know anything about your dad?'I asked.

Marcie smiled, her face lit up. 'He's famous,' she said, leaning back and staring at the sky.

'Famous?'

"Yes, all the Mums on the Estate know him. He's a traveller with the fair. His hair is black as a raven's wing and his eyes the colour of a summer sky. He's a free spirit that blows into town every August like a soft summer breeze. Mum says I get my wild ways from him. It's the gypsy in my soul.'

I remembered how I'd wanted to go to the fair. I'd asked Mum if she'd ever been. She'd sighed and said 'a long time ago.' She had that far away look in her eyes then too.

'But do you ever see him?' I said.

'I saw him last week at the fair. He treated me to all the rides. You should have come, he'd have treated you too.' Then she kicked her legs and swung really high.

Of course, you can't always believe what Marcie says. Mum says her tales are washed in a river of make believe, but she also said that sometimes all you have are your dreams and you shouldn't lose sight of them.

Still it proves one thing, my dad can't be Marcie's dad. Auntie Sarah doesn't know what she's talking about. 'Same seeds' indeed!

I kicked my legs and swung even higher than Marcie. Sometime I think I'm getting a bit too old for Marcie and her fantasies. A handsome traveller for a father – honestly, whatever next?

(First published in Woman's Weekly in 2014)

The Day Pops set his Trousers on Fire

'Mum rang,' Laura said, trying to sound as casual as she could with her jaws clenched.

'Oh?' There's nothing wrong is there?' Steve, her husband, said. Concern clouded his eyes. 'It's Pops' birthday next week. He's planning a barbecue.' Pops was Laura's grandfather and famous in the family for his dire culinary skills.

'Oh,' he said nodding with understanding. 'Well, it might not be so bad this time.' He gave her a hug.

Not so bad? It could hardly be worse than the last one, she thought. It was a few years ago now but she'd never forget it. It was one of those days that lodged in your memory like a bad smell in a small room...

It had been her twenty-ninth birthday and was Laura dreading it. Not the birthday, although twenty-nine sounded almost middle-aged, but her grandfather's insistence on having a barbecue to celebrate. She hated barbecued food, especially the inedible kebabs moulded with meat of indeterminate origin, seasoned to taste like minted lamb or the euphemistically called ranch house flavouring. The smoke always made her cough and her eyes water. Seeing her grandfather let loose with firelighters and matches set alarm bells clanging in her head. She visualised cremated sausages and burgers and chicken pieces charred to a cinder on the outside but a glutinous pink inside.

It was her birthday and she'd have preferred a sophisticated dinner party with a tasty roast, delicious desert, and generous helpings of cool crisp Chardonnay, accompanied by clinking glasses, lively conversations and lots of laughter, but Pops was so enthusiastic she didn't have the heart to refuse.

On the day the weather was gloriously hot, the garden blazed with colour, full blown roses bowed in the breeze their heady scent mingling with the smell of the fresh mown grass. Her dad rigged up the stereo in the garden so she could play her favourite music, the beer and wine flowed and soon everyone was enjoying themselves. Perhaps having a barbecue wasn't such a bad idea after all, she thought.

Then Pops noticed the absence of anything cooked on Laura's plate.

'You've nowt but salad,' he said. 'Here, let me help you.' He picked up a couple of sooty sausages with his tongs. Laura backed away. 'No really, I've had plenty. I guess I'm just not that hungry.'

'Nonsense. Growing lass like you. Come on now, what'll you have.' He glared at Laura.

'No, really, I'm off red meat. Cholesterol you know.' She beamed him her best smile but he wasn't to be defeated.

'I've got just the thing,' he said. He disappeared into the kitchen and returned with an ice-covered, glassy-eyed, trout straight out of the freezer. He placed it on the barbecue next to the oozing-fat burgers and blackened sausages.

'Won't take a minute' he called.

Laura watched in dismay as the melting ice sizzled onto the coals below, releasing clouds of smoke and turning the coals to grey ash. Pops' face fell.

Not to be deterred he went to the garage to fetch a blow-lamp which he lit directing its flames onto the now smoke-blackened fish. Under the intense heat the fish's skin blistered exposing pustules of pink flesh.

Encouraged by his success Pops tried to turn the fish over, wielding his tongs in one hand while wrestling with the blow-lamp in the other. The fish, its body all-but destroyed, fell apart; its head rested on the bars of the grill while its tail fell through to nestle on the coals. Half of its body remained in Pops' tongs while the rest disintegrated in a flurry of black skin and pink flesh.

Holding the half fish in mid-air he attempted to put the blow-lamp on the nearby table. Perched precariously on the empty fire-lighter box, it toppled. As it fell the flames caught the leg of Pops' trousers, then it lay on its side shrivelling the grass in a black line to the base of the fence.

Pops' trousers smouldered. He yelled, jumped backwards and flung the fish into the air. It spun in an arc and landed on the lawn in front of the barbecue where it was pounced on by next door's cat.

Pops continued dancing around in circles, hopping from foot to foot as his trousers gently smouldered until Ben, Laura's brother, with a rare flash of inspiration, scooped a bucket of water, from the rainwater barrel and threw it over Pops. Reeling sideways from the shock of the cold smelly water, Pops careered into the barbecue sending it crashing to the ground, scattering still hot coals over the flowerbed and setting light to the parched herbaceous border. The cat, alarmed by the shower of sparks, screeched and jumped at Laura, plunging its claws into her new Stella McCartney frock.

Laura screamed. The cat's weight gradually pulled it earthwards accompanied by the sound of ripping fabric.

By this time the fire had reached the fence. Laura shuddered at the memory.

'Oh, come on. It wasn't that bad,' Steve chuckled. 'Anyway if it wasn't for the barbecue I'd never have met you.' He kissed the top of her head. 'My loss,' he said.

Laura smiled, her face softened. How could she forget that day he walked into her life turning it upside down. Gut-wrenchingly handsome in his fireman's uniform, she'd fallen faster than a rock down a well. As soon as she gazed into his chocolate brown eyes she was hooked and she'd never wanted to wriggle free since. Her heart swelled at the memory.

'Hmm,' she said, snuggling closer to him, 'Perhaps a barbecue's not such a bad idea after all, but it might be best if you wear your uniform – just in case.'

(First published in Take a Break Fiction Feast in 2017)

A Brighter Tomorrow

Maggie could see the girl now, kneeling in the grass holding the sunshine yellow flower under her chin. It should have been a buttercup, of course, but at that age she hadn't known that. She supposed a bright yellow dandelion would do just as well. She'd been wearing her favourite blue and white checked dress, her auburn hair curled onto her shoulders. She must have been about five when she realised that her family was not like the other families in the village.

That was a lifetime ago. Since then she'd grown up, married a solicitor and had children of her own. She sighed. She couldn't go back, no matter how idyllic her childhood had been, but it didn't mean she didn't miss the happy times at Water's Edge, her family home.

Standing in the yard she gazed around. It looked unkempt. The dank smell of rotting leaves hung in the air. Pa would have hated to see it in such a state. A layer of dirt discoloured the old oak table and benches where they used to sit on long summer evenings. Her dad would light the barbecue and cook their meal, then they'd eat sitting around the table staying out until dusk fell and the sun spread its amber glow across the sky. A kaleidoscope of memories engulfed her – the kitchen garden her mum was so proud of, which had kept them fed, the barn where they played, the cowshed and the chicken run, all deserted. It would have to be put up for sale.

She glanced up at the house. It looked so different now. Then it had been full of noise and laughter. Tears too. There were always tears – still, she supposed that was what came with fostering – the excitement of arrivals followed by the heartaches of departures. She'd asked her mother about it once. "Don't you get attached?" she'd said.

Her mother had smiled her magical smile, and said, "I never forget they are other people's children. I'm just privileged to have them for a while to look after then send them on to bring happiness and joy to someone else. That's their role in life and mine."

She unlocked the door and walked into the house. Her footsteps echoed on the bare boards. The wallpaper was peeling and there were knocks in the paintwork where the removers had caught the woodwork while removing the furniture. The overall effect was dark and dismal. Nothing like she remembered. Her mum had moved into a nursing home over a year ago to spend her last few months being cared for. Maggie could hardly believe how quickly the place had deteriorated. Still, it had been a while since she'd visited. As she walked around the memories came flooding back.

The kitchen had always been the heart of the home. She took a breath. The room smelled musty with age. The once bright, colourful curtains hung, faded and torn at the grimy window. The vivid array of pots and jars that used to line the shelves was gone, along with the smells of fresh bread baking, or meat cooking that used to permeate the air. She shivered in the cold. What would her mother think? The only piece of furniture remaining was the heavy farm table in the centre of the room. Around this table they learned manners and how to wash their hands before eating, especially if they'd been out with the animals; lessons learned more readily by some than others. It was on this table Ma used to roll out the pastry for the pies she made to sell in the village to augment their meagre income. If Maggie was really good she'd be allowed to help.

She pictured her mother standing by the old iron range. It was how she always thought of her, busy in the kitchen, wearing her flowery apron which, like her hands, was usually covered in flour. It should have been called her floury flowery apron. The thought made her smile. She could never recall seeing her mum sitting down. She was always on the go, baking, scrubbing, polishing, but always smiling. When Maggie was that small child in the garden Ma had seemed like the font all wisdom. What would she say now?

"Can't live in the past," she'd say. "That way you might miss out on a brighter tomorrow." She was right of course. It was no use wishing your life away or agonising over things you can't change.

The only bits and pieces left in the house were the things that were too old or too personal to be of value to anyone else. Maggie would have to make arrangements to have them moved. At least the house had value. Life-changing money was how the Estate Agent had described it.

"Sell up and go on a cruise," he'd said. "Might as well enjoy what you have."

Maggie walked around the bare rooms. Cold and unwelcoming they felt now, whereas once they were warm and filled with love. Her mind spiralled back to the children her parents had fostered. There must have been almost two hundred over the years. One or two were babies awaiting adoption, but most were older and more troublesome, taken in for varying reasons and differing lengths of time. All were vulnerable and confused, defeated by the difficulties of their young lives but soldiering on because there was no option. Maggie's parents gave them all the same love and encouragement that Maggie received.

"We both had a poor start in life," her mother told her, when she asked why they took in so many waifs and strays. "We wanted to give them a better start than we had," she'd said.

As she walked around Maggie recalled the children's faces and their voices, so many children. She thought of them, playing in the yard, often squabbling and fighting, but she also remembered the laughter and huge affection.

She wandered into the front room. This was the room where they'd gather around the fire blazing in the grate when it was too wet or too cold to out. They'd sit reading or watching TV but only if they'd finished their homework, done on the dining room table under Maggie's dad's watchful eye. He had a heart a big as the barn. Always jolly and easy-going, he was the sort you could talk to if you had a problem. He'd stroke his chin and help you sort it out, never making any judgement; just helping you decide what you needed to do. He was the one made sure they all had a good education. No skipping school or not doing your homework. After school, those old enough helped out with the animals. Animals could get through to the most diffident, awkward or sullen kids where adults failed. Maggie recalled one boy in particular. Tommy his name was. He was a rumpled child with wide blue eyes and tousled sandy hair. He was twelve when he came to them – fifteen when he left. Tommy didn't speak for a week after he arrived. Slowly and surely Ma and Pa drew him out but only with the help of Horace, the dray horse that pulled the cart.

In the downstairs back room a pot of lavender had been left by the french windows. Her mum used to put lavender in all the rooms for the children, "to make them feel at home," she said. Her mother's rickety old desk stood in the corner. It was obviously too fragile and decrepit for the removers to take. On it she saw a pile of photo albums that had seen better days. They'd also left a chair and several boxes of papers on the floor. These were the things she'd have to sort out. She'd take them home with her and go through them. It would take time, she was aware of that. Everything else had gone; the Estate Agent had taken care of it all.

She sat on the chair and lifted the album off the top of the pile and ran her hands over the soft red leather cover with *'Photographs'* embossed in gold.

It smelled musty. She opened it and gradually turned the pages. Ma had kept photos of all the children they'd fostered. Seeing their pictures now, some over thirty years old, Maggie's heart fluttered. These were the living reminders of her childhood – the people she'd grown up with, her family. Each page brought a fresh wave of memories flooding over her. Here was little Billy, always in trouble in school, always getting into fights. How well she remembered her parents being called up to the school on numerous occasions to defend him. "One more chance," they'd say. "Just give him one more chance," and the headmaster always did. Billy grew from a troubled teenager to a fine young man. He joined the army and wrote to them from his postings all over the world. He'd come home to Maggie's dad's funeral five years ago. "He's the only dad I ever knew," he said.

Then there was Stephen, a bright lad pictured with Maggie's dad. His eyes shone with pride as he held up the cup he's won at the May Fair. He'd arrived when he was nine, stayed until eleven, then came back again at thirteen when his mother couldn't cope with him. He was a Barrister now, one of her parent's success stories.

Not everyone went on to avoid a life of crime but a great many did. There was Jack, a difficult boy, a bit backward with his speech and learning. The bewilderment in his six year old eyes when he arrived would make the hardest heart crumble. He didn't speak much either but their collie Dusty adopted him and would follow him around. He was the only one she'd settle with or allow to pet her. Jack could have ended up in prison like his dad, but he went on to discover a passion for carving. He married a local girl and found work in the stonemason's yard. They have three children now and a clutch of Dusty's puppies. He was at Maggie's mother funeral too. In fact the church was crowded with faces she remembered from the past.

One in particular had stopped and spoken to her. His name was Jimmy and he loved to play football, joining the local team when he was just fifteen. He spent so much time with the social workers it surprised no-one when he became one. Jimmy was a success story. He could so easily have been drawn into a life of drugs and alcohol that bedevilled his parents.

Maggie recalled all the boys and girls who'd passed though on their way from somewhere dreadful to, hopefully a better future. Maggie's parents said it was their job to get them fit to make the most of what life might offer, and that's what they did – every day of their lives.

Looking through the pictures that spanned a lifetime she wondered when her mother's hair turn into that cloud of white around her head and her face soften into the smiling granny face she had when Maggie saw her last.

Her dad too had turned grey and shrunk into the bones of an old man, but their hearts were as big as ever. They'd left the world a better place than they found it, that was for sure.

She put the album down. There were several more she could have gone through but outside the sky was darkening. She'd have to go home and get her husband's tea. Gazing out of the french-windows across the yard she could see the sun setting just as it always did, year after year, unchanging. This would be last time she'd be able to watch from the home she'd grown up in. Soon someone else would be enjoying the view.

She picked up the albums and carried them to her car, parked at the side of the house. Then there were the boxes lined up again the wall, boxes containing papers, letters and cards Ma had collected over the years. Maggie loaded them all into her car. I'll go through them at home, she thought, recalling all the letters, cards and flowers she'd had when her mum passed away, enough flowers for a May Day parade she'd thought. People were so kind.

As she locked the door behind her sadness filled Maggie's heart. She felt as though she was leaving her past behind and wished there was something she could do to preserve her parent's legacy and keep their memories alive.

Driving home Maggie thought more and more about her childhood. How different it was from many children's. Not everyone was blessed with a childhood bubble-wrapped in happiness. She thought of another child. One she'd shared her room with. Her name was Sarah, but everyone called her Princess. She was pretty as a princess with a riot of blonde curls that resisted all effort to tame them, a porcelain, doll like face and startling blue eyes. She followed Maggie's mum around like a lost puppy.

"I don't think I'll be here long," she'd say twenty times a day.

Maggie's mum would smile and say, "I don't suppose you will love, but while you are here I'm delighted to have you. Should we bake some cakes?"

Princess would smile and say "I might just stay for tea."

She was Maggie's age and in her class at school. "I don't think I'll be here long," she'd say every day to the teachers. After four years she stopped saying it and she and Maggie went on to senior school together. Last year Maggie saw her reporting the local news on TV, full of confident professionalism - a world away from the shy uncertain girl who arrives all those years ago.

When Princess did eventually leave she was replaced by Jenny, a much younger girl. Jenny didn't stay more than a few months, but Maggie saw her at her mother's funeral. She said she was training to be a doctor. Maggie wasn't surprised.

At home Maggie unloaded the boxes and carried the albums in. It would take some time to go through them and sort out the rest of her mother's estate. Hard to believe she'd been gone for over six months. Still, Maggie was in no hurry to pack away a lifetime of memories.

The next morning she called in at the Estate Agents to drop off the keys. She couldn't help but notice the brightness of the lights, the thick carpets, glossy brochures and smart, comfortable furniture, a stark contrast to her mother's house. She was greeted by the Agent's ever-smiling face.

"Are you ready for us to put it on the market?" he asked.

Maggie hesitated. Apart from the albums and boxes of papers it was all she had left of

her parents. "No," she said. "I'm not quite ready yet."

"Well, don't take too long. A property like that - it needs work. It's not everyone's cup of tea."

Over the next week Maggie went through the boxes. Every letter, card or photo brought another jolt of memory. Surely there must be something she could do to keep these memories alive.

The next evening she cooked her husband's favourite beef bourguignon and opened a bottle of wine.

"Are we celebrating?" Tom asked.

"I want your help and advice," Maggie said.

He frowned. "Go on."

"It's about Water's Edge. I've made enquiries. There's a desperate need for a safe place for troubled teenagers. I was wondering…"

"If we could restore it and open up the farm again as a respite centre?"

"Yes."

"We'd need to raise a bit of capital to fund it, pay for staff etc." He stroked his chin, just like Maggie's dad used to do. "We could set up a Trust I suppose and run it as a charity, but it would be huge undertaking, Maggie. You could be setting yourself up for a lot of heartache."

"That never stopped Ma and Pa."

Tom smiled. "I know. If it hadn't been for them I wouldn't be where I am today. It would be like giving something back, a worthy tribute too."

Maggie's heart leapt. She knew she'd made the right choice marrying Tommy, the fostered boy. He understood her passion for compassion.

Tom raised his glass, his wide blue eyes sparkled. "Let's drink to Water's Edge and a brighter tomorrow," he said.

Maggie clinked glasses. "A brighter tomorrow," she said, and her head filled with memories of all the children her mum and dad had fostered who could now work with her find that 'brighter tomorrow'.

(First published in People's Friend Magazine in 2016)

Roses for Remembrance

Alice surveyed the tangled mess that used to be Bob's garden, his pride and joy. He'd spend hours out there, cutting, planting and pruning. She sighed. She'd let it go. Six months now since the funeral and she hadn't even ventured out there. She blamed the cold, uninviting weather, the bare branches and frost-crusted grass appeared so desolate. The garden that used to bring such pleasure now only served to remind her of the depth of her loss, re-igniting the pain in her heart.

Spring beckoned. It was her favourite time of year. Bob loved the spring too with its promise of new life, golden daffodils and colourful tulips and iris. Alice heaved a sigh – she wasn't ready for a bright new life – she wanted the old one back; things the way they used to be.

She sighed again. She knew Bob wouldn't want her to be like this. He'd want her to get on with things and the make the most of the time she had left. Easier said than done, she thought.

She gazed out at the grass that needed cutting, the hedge that needed trimming and the flowerbeds that needed weeding. "Why don't you get someone in?" her daughter Sarah asked. "It wouldn't cost much to get someone to tidy it up."

But Alice couldn't bear the thought of another man taking Bob's place in the garden. It wouldn't be right. And what would the neighbours say? She didn't want anyone thinking she was trying to replace him, no one could do that. Anyway, they wouldn't do it the same as him – he had his own very firm ideas about gardening– things had to be done right. Set in his ways Alice used to say.

She smiled at the memory. That was one of the things she loved about him, his reliability. Predictability more like, Sarah said, but Alice loved that too. You always knew where you were with Bob. She didn't know where she was now he was gone, but she wouldn't be getting a man in to have the run of the garden that was for sure.

No – she'd do it herself. His tools were still in the shed. She'd do it just the way he used to.

The sight of the tools, pristine and orderly, jolted Alice back to earth. What on earth was she thinking of? She didn't know where to start, then she remembered his Gardening Magazine. It still arrived every month. She hadn't had the heart to cancel his subscription, it would be too final, like cancelling him out of her life.

Back indoors she swallowed her doubts and sorted through the magazines, opening the ones still in polythene. Inside she found the column headed 'Jobs to do this Month'. Great, she'd start there.

She began by cutting the grass. According to the magazine the state of the lawn set the tone of the whole garden. They'd bought a new hover mower last year, much easier to manage that the heavy old roller one you had to push. Well, that was a start. Alice hiked it out and began to mow. She found it a lot easier than she'd expected, just like putting the vacuum cleaner round, she thought. In fact, she quite enjoyed it. Next, she trimmed the hedges. The garden looked so much better she thought she might even tackle the weeds.

"If something grows where you didn't plant it – it's a weed," Bob used to say. Alice chuckled. She fetched the hoe and hoed up anything that looked as though it didn't belong. Once she'd finished she glowed with pride. He'd be proud of her too, she thought.

All through the summer she hoed, watered and weeded. She bought new plants from the Nursery to fill the gaps in the beds, choosing Bob's favourites. Sometime she found it difficult to keep up with all the jobs that needed doing, then she missed him more than ever.

One day, as she was working in the front garden, a man stopped at her gate. He raised his hat. "Good afternoon," he said.

Alice smiled. She recognised him from church. He came with a group of ladies from the sheltered housing a few streets away.

"I was just admiring your garden," he said. "It was always the best in the road, especially the roses, but I notice it hasn't been looking so well lately. I'm glad you've decided to spruce it up."

"Well," Alice said. "I'm not sure I'm doing that. I'm not sure what I'm doing at all."

He chuckled. "It looks to me as though you're doing a fine job," he said. "Can't beat a bit of gardening to chase the blues away." He raised his hat again and moved on.

The next Sunday he nodded to her in church.

"I didn't know you knew Harry," Alice's friend Betty said.

"I don't," Alice said.

"He used to have the big house on the corner of the Avenue, you know," Betty said. "Huge garden and he kept it lovely. Always out there he was, planting, tidying up, cutting and pruning. House was sold last year. I bet he misses it now."

Alice's heart turned over. She knew what it was like to miss something or someone you loved. Tears welled up in her eyes at the thought.

After that, whenever Alice was in the garden and Harry passed by he'd stop and admire the plants. "That lavender's a treat for sore eyes," he'd say. Or "I've haven't seen prettier geraniums this year." Alice saw the same gleam in his eyes that Bob used to get when he talked about his garden.

She smiled and nodded and wondered if she should invite him in for a cup of tea. Then she'd think better of it. Best to keep the fence between them, she thought. She didn't want anyone getting ideas.

Autumn arrived and, following the advice in the gardening magazine, she managed to sweep up the leaves and compost them. She was beginning to feel like a real gardener, until the weather turned damp and her knees started playing up and she found her back ached, then she'd think how pleased Bob would be and she'd carry on. Thoughts of him warmed her but then she'd be overwhelmed with sadness and a great swell of loneliness.

Each time she walked around the garden she recalled how Bob had planted rose bushes to mark milestones in their lives: Happy Event the day Sarah was born, Iceberg for their Silver Wedding Anniversary and Ruby Red for their fortieth. He took real pride in his roses. He'd won prizes for them. Now they looked straggly and in need of pruning. The magazine said this was the best time to do it. Alice had been fine with dead-heading them as the blooms faded but pruning was a different thing.

She checked the diagrams in the magazine and looked at the reaching-for-the-sky roses. There was no resemblance. Her heart fluttered. Supposing she did it all wrong and killed them? There'd be no prize winning blooms next year for sure. She thought about it for several days. Each time she gathered up her courage to step outside, secateurs in hand, her nerve deserted her. If she made a mess of it Bob would be spinning in his grave but if she didn't at least attempt it she'd feel a complete fool.

She did nothing about it until, one day she snagged her sleeve on a rose bush growing alongside the path and tore it.

That was it; she'd have to prune them now. She huffed and went to get the secateurs. She'd just raised her arm to make the first cut when Harry stopped at her gate.

"I wondered if you'd prune them," he said nodding at the rose bushes. "Best time to do it now. Cut them back hard for good growth next year."

Alice's heart sank. She really had no idea what she was doing. "Know much about roses do you then?" she asked.

He chuckled and raised his hat again. "Harry Budd, champion rose grower at your service," he said.

Relief flooded over Alice. "Do you think you could..." she waved her secateurs at the straggly bushes. "I've never done this before."

A wide grin spread across Harry's face. "I'd be delighted," he said.

Alice's heart pounded as she opened the gate. Was she doing the right thing? It was as if she were letting the rest of the world back into her life. What would Bob think?

Warmth flowed through her. He'd be happy that she was moving on, making a new life but keeping the old. "One is silver the other gold," Bob would have said.

A new found sense of peace settled in her mind as she opened the gate wide to let Harry in.

(First published in People's Friend Magazine in 2016)

If you enjoy these stories you might also like Kay's stories in **The Cappuccino Collection**. 20 stories to warm the heart, or **The Christmas Stories**, a special celebration of the magic that happens at Christmas in six short tales.

You may also enjoy Kay's Victorian novels:

The Water Gypsy
The Watercress Girls
The Guardian Angel

These three novels can be read together in **The Victorian Novels Box Set**, only available for Kindle.

If you have enjoyed Kay's stories she'd appreciate it if you'd add a review to help other readers find the books you enjoy so they can enjoy them too.

She'd also love to hear from you through her website: http://kayseeleyauthor.com/

Printed in Great Britain
by Amazon